TOTO'S TALE

An Adaptation of L. Frank Baum's
The Wonderful Wizard of Oz

SHANNON K. MAZURICK

authorHOUSE®

AuthorHouse™
1663 Liberty Drive
Bloomington, IN 47403
www.authorhouse.com
Phone: 1 (800) 839-8640

Published by AuthorHouse 04/27/2016

ISBN: 978-1-5246-0639-8 (sc)
ISBN: 978-1-5246-0638-1 (e)

Library of Congress Control Number: 2016906890

Print information available on the last page.

Dedication

This book is dedicated to my family and friends.

A Special Thanks

A special thanks is given to the loving animals in my life: past, present and future. It's also given to my kindergarten teacher and friend.

In Memory

This book is in memory of my dad.

Introduction

Toto's Tale (An Adaptation of L. Frank Baum's The Wonderful Wizard of Oz) is an adaptation of the classic story of The Wonderful Wizard of Oz. It is told from the perspective of Toto. Being that L. Frank Baum's The Wonderful Wizard of Oz is in the public domain, telling the story from Toto's perspective offers readers valuable lessons and provides an understanding of the importance to respect all living creatures.

Contents

Chapter 1

THE DRAIN OF THE SKY

Kansas was a dull and dreary place. The farm I lived on was a dusty and flat piece of land. I could see the land touch the sky in all directions. There wasn't one tree on the property. The sun could become extremely hot at times especially with my fur coat. It was tedious. The dust blew with the slightest breeze and stirred up with every step. Being that I was low to the ground, dust frequently was in my face.

The house was small. It provided the only shade from the sun. There was a kitchen and two bedrooms. The kitchen also had a door built into the floor leading down to a room under the house. The gentleman and his wife kept their bedroom door closed, as I liked to sneak in to nap on their big bed. They didn't like me on their bed and got mad when they caught me in there. However, in the kitchen, both of them would give me treats.

This couple was very mellow and low-key. I would refer to them as tiresome and boring people. They never seemed to have fun. For them, every waking moment seemed to be about work. Except for mealtimes and when they were sleeping, the couple did their best to take care of the farm. Everyday was repetitive for them. By watching the couple work, it was obvious that their zest for life had depleted. Life didn't seem to excite them and they didn't look for surprises. Their faces were wrinkly like pug dogs and their energy slowed as the day continued.

Dorothy, however, was different. She was a young lively spirit like me. The couple viewed Dorothy as odd. Dorothy would run around with me and play with me all day. She made Kansas a fun place. She had kindness in her heart and a sparkle in her eye. I enjoyed her spunk. We always woke up expecting surprises and had adventures daily. Dorothy always allowed me to sleep in her tiny bed. She would gently rub my belly every night until I fell asleep. As long as we were together, it didn't matter where we were; we made the best of it. I was Dorothy's dog, Toto.

Today I could sense that something was different though. As Dorothy and I were playing outside, Dorothy saw the couple standing frozen, looking out the door at the sky. Then, it was as if her playing stopped suddenly. The sky quickly darkened as I turned to look toward where the sky touched the land. With a loud noise, a drain appeared and it was moving closer. It reminded me of the water crate on the farm. When the water was drained and cleaned, there was a swirling. However, this drain was different. It was large and from the sky.

Dorothy swooped me up into her arms and dashed toward the house. As we entered the door, the couple went down into the room under the floor. The wind blew the floor door shut right before we reached it. Dorothy put me down to try to open the door. I felt the house shake so I scurried into Dorothy's room and squeezed under her bed. Dorothy came in, dragged me out, and carried me back into the kitchen.

Dorothy lifted the door open and a gust of wind hit our faces. The room under the floor was gone. The house was up spinning around in the drain of the sky. Neither Dorothy nor I could believe our eyes. Dorothy leaned over slightly. She probably wanted a better look; I knew I was curious as to what was happening. Suddenly, Dorothy's grip loosened around me as I peered through the door in the floor. I fell!

I thought I was a goner as I could barely see with the dust flying around. I did the only thing I could think of which was to do the doggy paddle swimming motion. It helped me when I was put in the barrel that was filled with water after I played with the pigs. The barrel was quite deep, and paddling my legs allowed me to keep my head above the water. This seemed similar as the ground was somewhere far below me. Luckily, paddling and the circulating air kept me up. Dorothy grabbed me as quickly as she could before I drifted away from the door in the floor. Once I was safe, she slammed the door shut.

After Dorothy sighed and I shook off, we went back into Dorothy's room and into her bed where we cuddled trying to wait out the storm. Despite all of the noise, the swaying of the house, and the wind, we somehow fell asleep.

Chapter 2

THE NEW TERRITORY

T hump! The bed flew in the air and landed back down. Dorothy and I bounced and almost hit the ceiling. Luckily, the mattress protected us because with a jolt like that, we easily could have been hurt. Waking up in midair is scary. Once I was confident that I was ok, I put my nose close to Dorothy's face. I had to make sure she was alright. As I rubbed my nose on her cheek, I whined as to ask what was happening.

I was a much lighter sleeper than Dorothy was and she was still half asleep after the bounce. As soon as my nose touched her skin and she heard me whining, Dorothy sprang up faster than ever. She glanced toward her window and it was obvious that she couldn't believe her eyes.

Sunshine filled the room. Somehow it was different. It seemed more refreshing this morning. Dorothy darted from bed to the front door and I dashed in the same manner close to her feet remembering how the drain in the sky picked up the house.

Dorothy gasped in amazement as she opened the front door. Her eyes opened wide and she put her hand toward her mouth. I scurried between her feet to see what was outside the door.

The house must have landed in a new place. I couldn't wait to explore this new land and from Dorothy's facial expression, I could tell she couldn't wait either.

The sun was warm and bright, but wasn't producing blazing heat. The air was pure and I could see marvelous color like never before. Soft green grass was everywhere. Trees were scattered. Each was full and had juicy looking fruit. Flowers were growing and spread out across the land. They were gorgeous. Colorful birds were heard singing and seen flying around in a playful manner. In the distance, a brook was seen with fresh water that sparkled. It was quite a beautiful sight after living on a Kansas farm.

For a second, Dorothy and I stood amazed taking in all the lovely sights. Then, I noticed people walking towards us and I began to bark. As they neared, I noticed that these people were all about Dorothy's height, however, seemed much older than Dorothy. There were three men and one woman. All of them were strangely dressed with rounded bottom pointy shaped hats with bells on them. The men had blue hats that matched their boots, pants, and shirts. The woman's hat was pure white that matched her dress. She sparkled like a star.

Star Lady approached us as the three men paused a few feet behind. She bowed in front of us. Dorothy smiled and I stopped barking. I could tell that these were nice people. Star Lady spoke softly in a sweet voice. She pointed to the corner of the house. Dorothy shook her head in fright. There was a person under the house. All that could be seen was the legs of the person with silver shoes. I went up to the sight and sniffed. The smell was horrible. It smelled like chicken poop. I shook my head and pawed my nose before rubbing my paw across the legs. There was no movement. The person was dead.

Star Lady gently took Dorothy's hand and led her up to the three men. I followed. By the way the men bowed in front of us and by the way they gestured evil looking actions followed by joyous actions, I could tell that the person under the house was evil and that the death freed the men.

Then, Star Lady pointed to the three men and then spread her arms wide to tell us that we not only freed the three men, but all the people of this new territory. I suddenly had the urge to explore this new territory in which I was quickly making my own by spreading scent simply by walking through the soft green grass. However, I remained by Dorothy's side.

Dorothy pointed at the three men, then at Star Lady, and then at the person under the house. Star Lady pointed at the three men and spread her arms out wide. I figured that the people of this new territory all dressed like the three men. Then, she placed both of her hands over her heart while holding onto a wand before pointing forward. I hadn't noticed the wand earlier, but I understood this to mean that she was a witch from a place in that direction. She then pointed straight behind her holding two fingers up.

This suggested that another good witch lived in that direction. Finally, still holding up two fingers, Star Lady pointed toward the person under the house, pointed at her wand again, and then pointed in the directions to her sides. I took this to mean that there were two wicked witches living in those directions, but one of them was now dead.

Dorothy seemed horrified at the thought that we were responsible for a death and the thought of witches among us. Star Lady and the three men smiled, praising Dorothy. They were ecstatic that one of the witches was dead and their happiness calmed Dorothy. I, however, was curious about the second wicked witch.

Dorothy soon questioned about the way home. The three men looked puzzled. I understood this as we did drop from the drain in the sky. Star Lady walked up to the corner of the house. The shoes were the only things remaining. Mysteriously, the body was gone. It did smell bad so maybe it simply rotted into nothing. Star Lady picked up the shoes and carefully placed them in Dorothy's hands. She gave Dorothy a gentle kiss on her forehead, which left a shiny mark. Then, she pointed to her wand before pointing toward a brick pathway. It was obvious that she was offering advice on how to figure out how to get home. She was telling us to see another powerful being of this new territory.

Just then, holding up her pointer finger, Dorothy sprinted into the house leaving Star Lady and the three men waiting outside. I followed Dorothy. Inside the house, amazingly not many of the belongings were disturbed despite all of the shaking from the drain in the sky. Dorothy packed a basket of food from the cabinets for the travels. Then, I followed her into her bedroom. She sat on her bed and looked at me. She gave me a pat on my head and I waged my tail. I knew she was glad I was sticking by her. It was because of me that she saw her shoes.

Upon noticing that her shoes were worn, she decided that the Silver Shoes were in better condition for the journey. Somehow they seemed to fit perfectly so Dorothy placed her other shoes in the basket. After taking one more look around the house, we went back outside, closing the door behind us.

Star Lady and the three men bid us goodbye as we started off on our travels. The three men waved. Star Lady gave a slight nod before spinning around on her left heel three times and disappearing into a cloud of white. Dorothy stared for only a split second before regaining her focus.

As Dorothy alerted me by calling my name, Toto, that we were to be on our way, I quickly realized that the rules of this new territory were very similar to the ones back in Kansas. My two main rules here were to behave and protect Dorothy.

Chapter 3

STRAW CHEW MAN

As we traveled along the brick pathway, the silver shoes on Dorothy's feet pinged with every step. Dorothy was walking quite fast. It was hard to keep up with her. It was obvious she was extremely eager to get home, but I was running with my tiny legs to stay by her side and I was starting to slightly pant.

There were nearby paths so we had to be careful not to stray from brick path. Although we were determined to get back to Kansas, it was impossible not to notice the beauty of our surroundings. It was a very pretty land compared to the farm back in Kansas. The sun was shining while clear blue skies filled the sky. Birds and butterflies fluttered around. Even though Dorothy and I were far from home, I could tell Dorothy felt it too. This place provided a sense of comfort and peace.

A few fences were passed along our way. Every one of them was painted blue. Multiple gardens grew on either side of the brick path. I figured that the people wearing blue had to be farmers.

Every so often we passed a house. The houses we passed so far were all painted blue with round roofs shaped like the hats of the people of this part of the land. The people came out to praise us and some even bowed as we walked by. It felt like everyone knew our purpose and our history about the house killing one the witches.

Continuing on our way, I could tell nightfall was soon approaching. I was getting tired keeping up with Dorothy's pace and she even looked tired. She still had determination in her eye, but noticing that the sky was darkening, she knew we needed to find a place to spend the night.

The next house we came across caught our attention. I could hear the music from a far distance away. As we approached, I saw a crowd of people dressed in blue dancing, laughing, and singing. A few were playing fiddles. A large table was covered with delicious smelling food such as meats, cakes, and pies.

Dorothy cautiously walked up to the crowd of people. They definitely were celebrating. I followed Dorothy with knowing that the people wearing blue that we had encountered thus far were all nice from what I could gather. I hoped these people were kind.

Once Dorothy and I were spotted, everyone threw their arms in the air and greeted us with excitement and gratitude. An elderly man called me on to his lap. I didn't see any danger. I rested my paws on his lap, as Dorothy was meeting everyone, grabbing a bite to eat, and dancing. Dorothy was never out of my sight, although I remained on the lap of this gentleman.

The man stroked me with one hand as he hand fed me goodies with his other hand. I was amazed how quickly the news spread about us, but I was certainly enjoying how these people wearing blue were treating us.

A little later on, the celebration started to quiet down as some people left. Fearful about us needing to spend the night outside in this new land, Dorothy asked about a place to spend the night. I knew this because she put her hands together and rested her head on her hands.

Without hesitation, the people smiled and gestured that we were more than welcome to spend the night with them. Looking confused, Dorothy picked me up. Noticing Dorothy's confusion of the kindness, the people seemed to try to explain. They pointed at her Silver Shoes, the kiss mark on her forehead, and curiously her dress. Her dress was blue and white. Dorothy put me back down on the ground and smiled. Suddenly, I understood. Of course, the Silver Shoes and the kiss mark had some magical powers. Then, the color white must represent goodness. Star Lady wore white. The color blue was the color of the people in this part of the land. Dorothy's dress had both colors so that explains their friendliness towards us.

One kind woman led us into the house and guided Dorothy by the hand to a bedroom. I stayed close to Dorothy. The room was decorated in blue and smelled of flowers. Dorothy slipped under the sheets on the bed and I jumped up onto the bed to curl up next to her

Before I knew it, it was morning. Dorothy made the bed and tidied up before leaving the room. The people of the house made us a breakfast as filling as the food the previous night. Dorothy and I could not have been more grateful.

After breakfast, Dorothy hugged each member of the household and we started back on our way. The day was similar to the one before so we walked at a steady pace after getting a good night sleep.

After walking quite a distance farther, I stared up at Dorothy as I noticed her slowing down. She looked back at me before sitting down on a tree stump next to a fence along side of the pathway. She took a piece of bread out of the basket for us to share.

It was nice to rest and take in the lovely sights of our surroundings for a minute. The fence surrounded a cornfield. In the center of the cornfield, a man attached to a pole looked over the corn and faced us.

It was a straw chew man. I had a couple toys back in Kansas that looked similar to him. Dorothy used to play with me as we both pulled on a straw chew man and shook it. The straw frequently flew out and scattered as we played. Dorothy just stuffed it back in making them as good as new. Back at home, larger straw chew men guarded the crops of the farm and scared away crows plus other animals by resembling a person. This straw chew man was dressed entirely in blue with a rounded bottom pointy shaped hat with bells on it. The people in this part of the land must have made him.

After finishing her piece of bread, Dorothy leaned her chin on the palm of her hand as her elbow rested on her thigh. She was in deep thought. She wanted to get back home. I could see it in her face. I felt bad so I went back to looking at the surroundings. Just then, Straw Chew Man winked.

Dorothy and I stared at each other in confusion. Then we looked back at the man. As we did, he nodded and smiled at us in a kind way. Dorothy stood up, climbed over the fence, and ran to the man. I did the same except I simply hopped through the fence.

Once we reached the man, we were stunned to learn that our eyes were not playing tricks on us. The man could move and he could speak as well. This land was not like Kansas.

As I was wondering the same thing, Dorothy must have asked Straw Chew Man if he was able to get down because she pointed downward. The man shook his head no. Before I knew it, Dorothy walked behind the man and lifted him off the pole.

Suddenly I couldn't control myself as Straw Chew Man was flopping in front of me to get use to being off of the pole, I grabbed a hold of his leg and tried to chew. It was very enjoyable to think of him as a giant toy.

Surprisingly, the man could walk too. As he ran to get away from me, chased him. I thought of it as a game until Dorothy grabbed my collar and yelled, "No". I knew I was wrong, but it sure was fun. I didn't hurt Straw Chew Man either. Straw was great for toys, although I quickly learned Straw Chew Man was not a toy. He dusted himself off and patted my head as he giggled. He seemed to have a little fun as well.

As we walked back to the brick pathway, I could tell that Dorothy invited Straw Chew Man to come with us. From the way the corn was half eaten, I could tell Straw Chew Man couldn't figure out how to scare the crows away from the corn. With straw packed into his head, I doubted that there was much room for brains.

Once we were back on the brick pathway and on our way, Straw Chew Man took the basket from Dorothy to carry it for her. It was then that I knew Straw Chew Man was a good boy.

Chapter 4

METAL MAN

Traveling along the brick pathway was nice with Straw Chew Man. It felt good to have someone from this land walking with us. However, while we traveled, the surroundings were starting to change. We passed fewer houses and fewer fences. The birds and butterflies were spotted less and less. Trees were becoming more frequent and as the sun began to set again, the trees started to cast shadows.

Dorothy didn't want to go any farther when the shadows grew larger. I wasn't scared. Dorothy stopped walking and looked very frightened to proceed ahead. Trying to show her that there wasn't anything to fear, I ran a few feet ahead of Dorothy and barked for her to follow. Straw Chew Man offered to hold Dorothy's hand, but she obviously didn't want to go much farther with nightfall once again approaching.

Straw Chew Man and I surveyed the area with our eyes. I spotted a small house in one direction not far from the brick pathway. I barked and Straw Chew Man pointed to the house. Dorothy had a big bright smile.

We went up to the house. It was a light blue house with a metal roof. Inside the house was dark. Dorothy rang the doorbell and knocked. Nobody appeared to be home. Disappointed, she walked up to a pile of leaves in the yard.

Dorothy was very tired so she fell asleep on the pile of leaves. Straw Chew Man didn't seem tired and actually seemed to be energetic at all times. He was willing to wait quietly until we woke the next morning so I fell asleep next to Dorothy.

When morning arrived, a light shinning right on our eyelids woke Dorothy and me up. Rubbing her eyes, Dorothy sat up. Standing only a yard away from us, a man stood. I leaped to my feet and barked. Dorothy quickly stood up.

The man was holding up an axe as he faced a tree. The man wasn't moving. I wanted a closer look. I was curious, but Dorothy didn't dare go near the man and she screamed my name. Even with her screaming, the man didn't show any movement.

As I inched my way closer to the man, I realized that the shining that woke us up was the sun reflecting off the metal. The man was entirely made of metal. Once the man didn't move as I sniffed his feet, Dorothy and Straw Chew Man came closer.

Dorothy put her hand on her cheek in amazement that the man was made of metal. The position he was in with the axe in mid-swing was rather odd. In fact, seeing a metal man in front of an empty house was strange. As Dorothy admired the facial molding of the metal, a moan was heard. Dorothy jumped back. The moan sounded like a mouse back in Kansas when it was stuck in a metal bucket. It was very soft.

Dorothy, Straw Chew Man, and I all looked at each other with wonder. Being that he was hooked on the pole since his creation, Straw Chew Man probably was as amazed as us to hear a man made of metal moan.

Then, I spotted a can on a nearby tree stump. Back in Kansas, similar cans were used to keep equipment and certain tools in working order. I barked once to get Dorothy to look my direction. It worked and she saw the can. She patted my head, smiling, before picking up the can.

Dorothy dripped the contents of the can over all of the possible moving parts of the metal man. Soon, Metal Man was talking and moving with ease. He was alive just like Straw Chew Man.

He repositioned the axe so he was carrying it with the sharp part towards the ground. Then, he tapped on his chest. A loud hollow echo sound was heard. The sound was his way to show us that he didn't have a heart.

I had a feeling that Metal Man lived here all alone and that he didn't have any friends. That explained the metal roof on the blue house. Metal Man must have got stuck in a storm while trying to chop wood and it made him freeze in place.

Metal Man seemed extremely grateful that we helped him. Dorothy being a kind soul felt sympathy for Metal Man after learning he was missing a heart. I think all three of us felt badly for him when we realized he was created without a heart. Dorothy gently took his hand and invited Metal Man to join us on our journey. He nodded and gave a sweet smile. We were once again on our way.

Chapter 5

BIG CAT

The road remained shady for quite a distance. Trees casted shadows and let little light through. Broken branches and dry leaves were scattered across our path. I had to be careful not to scratch my paws. Every so often, I heard things. When I stopped the first few times to listen, the noise went silent. I was positive I heard something, but Dorothy wanted to continue our travels.

A little while later, we all heard growling and leaves rustling. It sounded like someone was following us. I walked close to Dorothy. Another growl followed. We all stopped and I listened, but didn't bark. Dorothy picked me up and walked briskly along the road. I could feel her heart pounding as she held me close to her chest.

Suddenly, a creature leaped out in front of us. It was a big cat. I wasn't scared of cats so I began to bark. Big Cat started crying and hid behind a tree. I stopped barking. I had protected Dorothy! I was proud of myself!

I thought we would continue on our way, but Dorothy could not leave someone crying. We slowly approached Big Cat and Dorothy crouched down beside him with me still in her arms. Big Cat watched as Dorothy stroked me. Before I knew it, Big Cat was joining us on the journey.

However, it was getting dark again so we decided to find a place to rest for the night. As Metal Man gathered wood to build a fire, Big Cat went into the woods and brought back a deer. Dorothy, Big Cat and I were hungry, but Metal Man had a hurt look on his face. It was obvious that he felt bad seeing that a living creature was killed. Metal Man started a fire because he knew we had to eat. Then, Metal Man and Straw Chew Man went off to gather more wood as we cooked the meat and ate. I could tell Straw Chew Man was eager to get away from the fire and Metal Man couldn't handle watching us eat. Being that we were hungry, it didn't take long for us to finish. They returned shortly afterwards. Straw Chew Man kept his distance from the fire, but the night passed by fast as we enjoyed each other's company.

As soon as daylight came, we were back traveling along the road. Soon, the shadows from the trees began to soften before they completely diminished. Lovely landscaping once again surrounded us. Straight ahead was a large sparkling wall. I knew that had to be where we were heading. With our eyes gazed on the sparkling, we quickly continued walking. All of a sudden, mice scurried beneath our feet breaking our focus. Big Cat chased straight ahead after them. He pounced catching one by its tail with his paw.

I also liked to chase mice, but I controlled myself this time since we were so close to reaching the place that could make our hopes come true. Dorothy picked up Big Cat's paw, releasing the mouse. Big Cat stepped back. The mouse, surprisingly, didn't run away. Instead, it looked up at Dorothy, nodded in thanks, and patted the ground twice before continuing on its way. I didn't give it much thought as we soon were in front of a large sparkling wall.

Chapter 6

THE GREAT
SPARKLING CITY

T he large sparkling wall shimmered with beauty. I almost didn't notice the flowers surrounding the great sparkling wall. They were rich in colors and smelled lovely. I, however, contained my want to roll in them and kept my concentration with Dorothy.

The large sparkling wall was so tall that we couldn't see what was behind it. I suspected that something wonderful was inside and the wall was for protection. Dorothy looked puzzled for a brief moment before noticing a single crack in the wall. Stepping back, we discovered that there was a huge door blending into the wall. Dorothy didn't hesitate to knock.

With a screech, the door opened just enough so a soldier with the cat-like whiskers could squeeze out before slamming the door close. It was obvious that this was a highly protected place. The soldier with the cat-like whiskers had black and white markings with a pointy nose. I didn't like how he examined each of us by sticking his nose in our faces while staring at us. When he came close to me, I lightly growled, which made him move on from me to examine Dorothy. Upon noticing her Silver Shoes and the shiny mark from Star Lady's kiss on her forehead, the soldier with the cat-like whiskers immediately took glasses out of his pocket and placed them over each of our eyes. I tried to paw them off, but it was no use. Then, the soldier opened the door entirely. Behind the sparkling wall was a great sparkling city.

The Great Sparkling City had a lively atmosphere with music, dancing, and cheerful people. Flowers were everywhere and as radiant as the ones surrounding the wall. Once inside, the soldier closed the door behind us before gesturing to us to follow him. As we followed, I noticed that everything was sparkling. Even the buildings, flowers, and people sparkled. It was a glorious site.

When we reached the front of the largest building of the Great Sparkling City, the soldier stopped, turning to face us. He held up his hand, signaling for us to stay. He entered the building leaving us waiting.

A few minutes later, the soldier with the cat-like whiskers let us in the building. We followed him to another doorway. This time, he opened the door and nodded his head sideways to tell us to enter. I could tell he was going to wait there until we returned.

The room was pitch black. We walked cautiously forward. Suddenly, a loud voice asked for our purpose for bothering him. Straw Chew Man answered first. A large fireball appeared directly in front of us. The heat from it was blazing hot. Straw Chew Man was horrified. As quickly as the fireball appeared, it was gone and the room turned dark. Metal Man then spoke. When he finished, a humongous melting head floated down, paused in front of us, and then the room went dark again. Metal Man was terrified. Next, with a little encouragement from Dorothy, Big Cat spoke. When he finished, a giant beast with fur, fangs, and horns appeared in front of us.

Big Cat fell to his knees in tears. I barked at the beast and the room went dark once again. Dorothy, then, stepped forward and spoke in a direct voice. The loud voice replied. Since Dorothy had her hand covering my ear pressing my head against her chest, I only heard the words grant, come, destroy, wicked, and witch. The loud voice must have told us that he would grant our requests, but we would first need to come back when we destroyed the Wicked Witch. Dorothy questioned why, but the loud voice yelled, "Go!"

I leaped out of Dorothy's arms and we all ran out of the room in fear. The soldier with the cat-like whiskers led us out of the building. Once outside, we all collapsed to the ground to catch our breaths. The soldier patiently waited for us to stand back up. He wanted to lead us to the exit of the Great Sparkling City, but Dorothy wouldn't follow him until he listened to her. She always meant business when she held her hand on her hip. The soldier sighed before complying. As Dorothy raised her hands to a point over her head and then pointed in different directions, the soldier had a confused look on his face as he listened. I knew she was asking for directions to the Wicked Witch. Despite the concern in his eyes, the soldier nodded and led us to the door of the wall. When we all were through it, he took the glasses off of our eyes placing them back in his pocket and once again he slammed the door behind us before gesturing for us to follow him. Dorothy picked me up again and held me close before following.

CHAPTER 7

THE WICKED WAY

The street, the soldier, the Great Sparkling City, the unfamiliar creatures, and even the way Dorothy clutched me to her chest seemed different. Dorothy's comforting words to me said one thing, but her hands were sweaty and her hold on me was a little tight. I saw in Dorothy and her friends' facial expressions, especially in their eyes, that they were afraid of what they would find on this journey. I could sense that we were heading into the lands of the Wicked Witch of the West. The lively atmosphere of the great sparkling city soon diminished. A gloomy fog grew thicker and flowers that surrounded the city thinned out the farther we traveled. The scent of the Wicked Witch was growing stronger as we followed the soldier with the cat-like whiskers from the Great Sparkling City to the home of another individual. Then, he nodded and returned to the city.

I liked this new animal. This one didn't seem as scared of me as the soldier did. He was short and pudgy with a slightly pushed in snout. His head was wrinkly and he reminded me of a bulldog. He must have been a direction-giver because he had a handful of maps in his hand. I also realized that the critter lived directly in the center of numerous paths. I knew he would be able to give us directions to the Wicked Witch. As soon as he spotted me, he stroked me and rubbed his nose against my cheek. It was nice to be adored, although I was on guard and couldn't let myself get caught up in the attention. I had to be alert so I could warn Dorothy and the others if any dangers were lurking. The creature soon turned his attention to Dorothy. She must have asked him which road led to the Wicked Witch of the West because he suddenly stopped petting me and curiously stared at her.

There were many roads leading in different directions. The woods, however, had the strongest scent of the Wicked Witch. She smelled like rotten eggs combined with the slop that the pigs ate back on the farm in Kansas. It was a terrible odor that could not be mistaken for anything else except for the Wicked Witch. For some reason though, Dorothy and the others weren't bothered by the stench. But I was, and I knew it was coming from the woods. Where was the road through the woods? There didn't appear to be one. I could tell that by the darkness in that direction that no one travels through the woods except for the Wicked Witch. From the way the critter reacted to Dorothy, I was pretty sure nobody ever comes out from the woods either, except for the Wicked Witch. I didn't know of any reason for anyone except for her to travel through the woods either. However, we weren't just anybody! We had a mission! The animal pointed to the woods and

Dorothy gulped. It was clear he didn't dare go near the woods, but by pointing, he told us to travel in the direction the sun sets.

I could tell by Straw Chew Man's movement that he was telling the direction-giver that we were planning to destroy the Wicked Witch. Straw Chew Man swung his arms and bounced around like he was boxing. Then, Metal Man joined in by lifting his axe and I couldn't help myself. I gave out a bark!

The direction animal wished us good luck and went back inside his house. As we walked towards the edge of the woods, Dorothy squeezed me tighter and tighter in her arms. I could tell by the way they walked, slowly with hesitation, that Dorothy and the other three who joined us along the way (Straw Chew Man, Metal Man, and Big Cat) were frightened.

Out of all my companions, I was the brave one. I wasn't scared. I was confident that I could protect them and frighten away the unknown. I let out another fierce bark, "woof," letting my companions know that their friend Toto would never leave their side. As we advanced, the ground became rougher and the woods were darker and more formidable. There were many sticks and rocks to navigate over. Metal Man would walk and when he stepped on a rock, the pinging sound was very loud and would echo through the woods. Dorothy stumbled a few times over the terrain. Every sound and rustle we heard made Dorothy shiver. I could hear her heart pounding faster and faster with each step she took as we traveled deeper into the woods. Big Cat jumped at everything and did not like the darkness of the woods. I became more anxious; the more the eerie sounds affected Dorothy. The trees appeared larger as we went deeper into the woods. The sunlight soon grew dim because it could not pass through the branches. The day seemed to turn into night, which made Dorothy, Big Cat, and me become tired.

We decided to rest since we had been traveling for a while. We found a special place that made me feel comfortable and safe. It was a patch of grass somehow growing in the thick woods and it seemed inviting so Dorothy, Big Cat, and I laid down for a nap. The other two companions kept a lookout for us as we slept.

A little while later, I was awakened by a high-pitched whistle. Dorothy and Big Cat were still sleeping. My ability as a dog to hear high-pitched sounds served me well. The whistle didn't disturb them. However, it made me jump to my feet. I knew that the whistle meant that something was about to happen so I had to alert the others. Straw Chew Man and Metal Man continued to stand guard. As I barked and nudged the two of them, the ground began to rumble. I heard growling growing louder and louder. A pack of wolves was heading towards us. They had long legs, fierce eyes and sharp teeth. I knew these weren't ordinary dogs. These were wolves looking for a fight. The whistle I heard must have been the Wicked Witch summoning the wolves. She must have sent the wolves to destroy us.

Straw Chew Man picked me up just as one of the wolves leaped out from behind a tree and headed straight towards us. He held me in his arms as Metal Man stood in front of us. I was so upset. I wanted to show these wolves just how tough I could be. All I could do was bark and struggle while Straw Chew Man had me in his arms. Although I knew that it was unlikely that Straw Chew Man would let me go, I continued to bark and squirm in an attempt to intimidate those wolves. However, they didn't seem that tough. Metal Man stood in front of us with his shiny axe. The wolves started attacking and Metal Man swung his axe, killing most of them before they had the chance to do any damage. Furthermore, when the wolves ganged up on him and attacked two or three at a time, Metal Man didn't panic. He swung his axe, killing one wolf at a time while the rest tried to hurt him by biting his legs. Since he was made of metal, the wolves broke their teeth as they gnawed on his legs. Then, the axe sliced through their necks and killed them.

Before I knew it, there was a bunch of wolves lying dead in a heap. Metal Man had killed the entire pack. I was disappointed that there wasn't one wolf left for me to fight because I had the duty of protecting Dorothy. However, as I looked at the bunch, I was glad that Metal Man was around because I would not have been able to fight off all those wolves by myself. It was then that I realized how sharp the axe was and I feared what the axe could do to me if it could slice through those wolves so easily. I was so much smaller than those wolves. I was glad I was traveling with Metal Man and that he liked me better than the wolves. When Metal Man was confident the battle with wolves had ended, he put down his axe and sat down in relief. Straw Chew Man put me down and sat down beside him.

Dorothy and Big Cat were deeply sleeping. Unbelievably the noise from the battle didn't wake them! It was as if their sleep was protected by goodness. I sniffed around their mouths to make sure they were alive. Both were breathing, although Big Cat's breath had a pungent smell. Metal Man and Straw Chew Man started patting the ground and whispering my name. I went over and lay down in front of them. They both started rubbing my belly. It felt so nice. It made my back leg move uncontrollably, which only happens on rare occasions when somebody pets me and I become all silly because it feels very good. I must have done something right in order to deserve such pampering. I soon realized that I had protected Dorothy after all by alerting Straw Chew Man and Metal Man that danger was lurking.

When Dorothy and Big Cat finally woke up, Dorothy gasped when she saw the great pile of dead wolves. I licked her hand to assure her that everything was alright. Big Cat didn't seem to care much. I had a feeling that he was afraid of most living creatures in the woods, but dead animals did not frighten him. After all we met him while cutting through the patch of woods just before we made our way to the Great Sparkling City so he knew dead animals were not to be feared. Dorothy, however, was very grateful that we protected her from the pack of wolves. She thanked each one of us with a hug. She even kissed me on the head.

After we celebrated our victory, we continued on our journey. We only traveled a short distance before I heard that high-pitched whistle again. The Wicked Witch must have been watching us and decided to send more trouble our way since we survived the attack by the wolves. I barked and started climbing up Dorothy's leg to warn her that danger was coming. Metal Man and Straw Chew Man understood my warning signal. They stopped cautiously to make sure there weren't any signs for concern. Before I knew it, a great flock of crows were flying right towards us. There were so many crows and they all were swooping down at us together. Straw Chew Man gave us a hand signal to lay down beside him so Dorothy grabbed me and laid face down on the ground with her arm sheltering me. Big Cat and Metal Man laid down on the opposite side of Straw Chew Man, as well. Straw Chew Man bravely stood up and stretched out his arms. I was able to see what was happening with one eye. I couldn't miss the excitement by lying down with my eyes covered. It was bad enough that Dorothy wouldn't let me help fight off the crows. I had to know what was going on. When the crows saw Straw Chew Man stretched out, they were frightened, as crows always are by straw men like him, and they did not dare to come any closer. They perched themselves on the surrounding tree branches and just stared at him. The King Crow must have thought Straw Chew Man was harmless like the Kansas crows learned Kansas scarecrows are harmless, because he flew straight at him. Straw Chew Man sure gave him a surprise, though. He caught him by the head and twisted his neck until he died. The other crows soon became angered that the King Crow was dead and started flying towards Straw Chew Man one at a time. Straw Chew Man continued to twist their necks, until they lay dead at his feet. After all the crows were dead, Straw Chew Man confirmed that it was safe to get up, but I double-checked by sniffing their carcasses. When Dorothy and the others finished dusting off their knees and thanking Straw Chew Man, we continued on our journey.

A little while later, I heard that high-pitched whistle for the third time. I barked again to warn my companions of danger emerging. This time everybody understood that my barking was a warning. Dorothy picked me up as we both listened to hear if something was approaching. Soon enough, buzzing filled the air and a swarm of black bees was flying toward us. Straw Chew Man once again signaled to Dorothy and to Big Cat to lie face down. This time Dorothy held me close to her body as she sheltered me with her arm. Then, Straw Chew Man took out his straw and scattered it over us. The straw was hot and itchy. Luckily, we didn't have to stay under it very long. I heard a few pings and before I knew it Metal Man confirmed that it was safe to get up. I verified that we were safe by quickly running over and smelling the bee parts. The bees must have tried to sting Metal Man because they were lying dead in a pile with broken stingers. Dorothy and Big Cat helped Metal Man gather up the straw so they could put it back in Straw Chew Man. I helped sniff out every piece of straw to make sure not a single piece was missed. When Straw Chew Man was whole again, we continued on our journey.

From then on, our travels seemed to go smoothly. I didn't hear a whistle for quite some time and I thought the Wicked Witch had run out of ideas on how to destroy us. I was wrong. She changed her approach. A little while later, I started hearing footsteps in the distance, although I didn't hear a whistle. The footsteps were coming closer so I stopped and barked once. The others became very quiet and listened. A bunch of raccoon-faced creatures dressed in funny yellow furry uniforms and carrying sharp spears were approaching us. Just as they were about to attack us, Big Cat gave out a loud roar and sprang toward them. The raccoon-faced beings were obviously not brave creatures. They ran back in the direction they came from as fast as they could when they heard the roar. The roar didn't frighten me. Big Cat was trying to protect us, but I have the feeling that even though the raccoon-faced creatures were carrying spears, they would have been spooked by any little danger aimed towards them. My growl probably would have made them react the same way. As far as I could comprehend, the raccoon-faced creatures had to be slaves or prisoners of the Wicked Witch and they had to do as they were told or they would be punished. I wondered what the Wicked Witch would do to them when they returned unsuccessful. However, we were certain that the raccoon-faced creatures would not return to us so we continued on our journey.

As we got closer to the Wicked Witch's castle, her stench became very potent. We had to be close. I knew she wouldn't let us reach her castle without one last attempt to kill us and since she didn't seem to be using the whistle anymore, I was on high alert. We had survived everything the Wicked Witch attempted to destroy us with so far. Therefore, I figured she was going to resort to desperate measures. She needed things to go her way and it must have upset her when her other plans failed.

Suddenly, just as we left the woods, the refreshing sight of a clear sky was gone. The sky filled with dark clouds and I heard a low rumbling sound from above. Cackling was heard close by as the winds blew strongly, making it difficult for me to see because of the pine needles and dust blowing around. A few minutes later, the sun came out of the dark sky to reveal the Wicked Witch standing outside her castle, surrounded by a bunch of flying monkeys.

One of the monkeys was much bigger than the others and seemed to be the leader. On the Wicked Witch's command, the monkeys started flying towards us. Dorothy scooped me up and tried to escape, but they cornered us on the edge of a steep rocky incline. Dorothy held me tight against her chest. I could hardly breathe. Just as one of the monkeys was about to push us over the edge, he stopped and took a step backwards. Dorothy dropped down on her knees, which almost made my breakfast reappear because she pushed in on my stomach as she fell to the ground. Other monkeys gathered around us to see what the problem was and why we weren't destroyed as the Wicked Witch wanted. They were right in our faces. I almost gagged because their breath smelled like rotten bananas and sour milk. I knew something was going on though, because the monkeys were staring at Dorothy as though she possessed a power that they didn't want to mess with. They kept pointing at her forehead where Star Lady kissed her and at the shoes Star Lady gave to her when we first arrived in this new land. Straw Chew Man and Metal Man were tortured though. Two winged monkeys flew over us, as they carried away Metal Man. Then, they dropped him on the rocky surface behind Dorothy. We could just watch and listen as Metal Man hit the pointy rocks and his shiny, smooth metal became severely dented. Then, four winged monkeys lifted Straw Chew Man into the air and pulled him apart by his limbs. They scattered Straw Chew Man's stuffing across a dense and wide patch of the woods. Dorothy's eyes filled with tears as she watched these horrific events happen right in front of her. For the first time I didn't know how to comfort Dorothy. It was hard to see her so upset and not be able to do anything to make her feel better. I leaned up and licked her chin. It was the

only thing I could think of, but it just made her cry harder and squeeze me tighter.

Once the lead monkey made sure that Metal Man and Straw Chew Man had been incapacitated, he approached Dorothy and me to decide what to do with us. He took a good look at Dorothy's forehead as well as her shoes. I was shaking because I thought we were done for, but luckily he just turned around and nodded to the other monkeys. At that point, I knew our lives were spared at least from the monkeys.

The lead monkey kindly helped Dorothy to her feet and grinned as two other monkeys hovered over us. Carefully and gently they lifted Dorothy in their arms and up into the air. I couldn't help shaking, although Dorothy still held me tight in her arms. We were very high up. However, as I looked down, I could see the remaining monkeys throwing pieces of rope around Big Cat until he was unable to bite, scratch, or struggle. I was wondering what happened to him! I'm glad the monkeys didn't hurt him and I knew Dorothy would be happy to know he was unhurt. I softly nudged Dorothy with my head to show her that Big Cat was unharmed. She spotted him just as he was being lifted into the air and carried in the same direction we were headed.

CHAPTER 8

THE WICKED WITCH

T he monkeys carried us to the Wicked Witch's castle, where they placed us gently down on the front door step. Big Cat followed. He was not deposited on the front step with us. Instead, the monkeys placed him in a small iron fenced in yard and untied him. The fence was high and the gate latch had a key lock. Escape didn't seem possible.

The leader of the Winged Monkeys then flew up to the door and knocked. When the Wicked Witch answered, her eyes became narrow when she saw us at her door. She was displeased to learn that we were alive, but when the monkey pointed at Dorothy's shoes and at her forehead, the witch began to tremble with fear. However, the Wicked Witch shook the monkey's hand when she heard that her other commands had been obeyed. I could tell that the monkey was explaining how the other wishes were followed by the way the Wicked Witch was smirking and from the gestures the monkey made as he spoke. Also, I gathered from the horse-like gestures exchanged between the monkey and the Wicked Witch that the witch planned to tame Big Cat to the point where she would be able to ride him like a pony. The witch was pleased with what the monkeys had accomplished and seemed to understand why they didn't harm Dorothy or me. She bid the monkeys good-bye and then all the monkeys flew into the air and were soon out of sight.

With the monkeys' departure, Dorothy and I were left staring the Wicked Witch in the face. I could tell that at first the witch was tempted to run away from Dorothy by the way she backed up every time Dorothy inched towards her. Fear was in her eyes. It was amusing. However, a smirk ran across her face as she glared at Dorothy. I knew the shoes Dorothy was wearing and the kiss from Star Lady must have had great power if the monkeys and the witch didn't harm us yet. The smirk across the Wicked Witch's face and the way she was looking at Dorothy made me concerned, though. Dorothy nor I knew how to use her powers, which worried me. We had made it this far so there had to be a very strong power protecting us associated with the shoes Dorothy was wearing and the kiss on her forehead from Star Lady.

The witch stepped aside, allowing us to enter her castle. The door startled me as it slammed shut as soon as we were inside. Dorothy held my head against her chest and I could hear her heart pounding as she followed the witch into the kitchen. I wondered what the witch had planned for us. The witch placed an empty bucket and a mop in front of Dorothy. Then she pointed to the kitchen floor. She was going to make Dorothy into her maid. Scared of the consequences if she didn't obey the Wicked

Witch's every command, Dorothy put me down and filled the bucket with water from the sink. It broke my heart to see Dorothy doing chores for the Wicked Witch. Dorothy didn't deserve to be treated this way. I had to figure out a way to free Dorothy and Big Cat.

While Dorothy filled up the bucket with water, I noticed that the witch scurried out of the kitchen. Why was she leaving in such a rush? I decided to follow her. Dorothy was busy washing the kitchen floor so I figured she would be alright for a few minutes. I followed the witch as she went into a tiny shed where she filled a bowl with food. She carried the bowl out to the fence where Big Cat was trapped. She grabbed the key hanging on a tree and opened the gate latch after placing the food out of Big Cat's reach. She walked in, closing the gate behind her. When the witch leaped and tried to get on top of the back of Big Cat as if he was a tamed horse, he roared fiercely, scaring her. Fearing for her safety, the Wicked Witch ran out of the gate and locked the latch again. In disgust, she flipped her hair over her shoulder and was heading towards the castle taking the food with her. I could see that the Wicked Witch was planning to starve Big Cat until he agreed to let her ride him. This upset me terribly. Starving somebody in order to improve their behavior is wrong. I knew that I wouldn't like it if I wasn't fed. Unfortunately, I couldn't do much about the situation at the moment because I needed to get back to Dorothy to make sure she was alright. Nevertheless, I was determined to make sure Big Cat didn't go hungry.

Over the next couple of days, Dorothy continued to do the chores that the witch had assigned to her. She swept the floor, kept the fire fed with wood, and dusted the entire castle. Dorothy worked as hard as she could to obey every command to the best of her ability. She also did the tasks with a smile. This surprised me at first. I didn't know how Dorothy could keep a smile upon her face throughout the day in such a difficult situation. However, since she didn't know as I did that the witch was extremely frightened by the power Dorothy possessed, she was thankful the Wicked Witch had decided not to kill her. At night, Dorothy's true emotions showed and she cried for many hours.

She cried over the last time we saw Metal Man and Straw Chew Man. It upset her to think about what happened to them. She also cried over her fear of our future and cried about her want to return to Kansas. I shared her sadness. I would sit at her feet and look at the tears run down her face. I whimpered as Dorothy cried, trying to show Dorothy that I didn't like to see her upset and to let her know I felt confident that changes for the better were coming soon. I did not care whether I was in Kansas or in this new land as long as Dorothy was with me, but I knew Dorothy was unhappy, and that made me unhappy too. I needed to find a way to defeat the Wicked Witch. She was the cause of Dorothy's unhappiness and she had to be killed.

I couldn't figure out how she could be destroyed, although I began to notice that she stayed away from water. When Dorothy mopped the castle floors or when water was being used, the witch kept her distance. I decided to knock over the water bucket the following morning. Unbeknownst to the witch, Dorothy and I had been sneaking food to Big Cat every night while she was sleeping, and now, she was becoming more and more frustrated that her plan was not working. She stormed into the castle like clockwork every morning while Dorothy mopped the floor, frustrated that Big Cat continued to refuse to let her ride on his back. The witch took out her frustration on Dorothy and me when she returned from checking on him. The witch made us work harder and gave us nothing to eat. Each day she was becoming more hot-tempered. I was certain she would follow the same morning routine and I knew exactly what to do. I just hoped water would be the end of her.

The next morning, everything went according to plan. Dorothy filled the bucket with water as the Wicked Witch went out to check on Big Cat. A few minutes later, Dorothy had just started mopping the kitchen floor when suddenly I heard a "SLAM." It was so loud that my ears started throbbing. I barked aggressively, "ROOF" in the direction of the sound. I knew it had to be the Wicked Witch slamming the door, frustrated that her attempt to ride Big Cat had failed again and her smell was starting to burn my eyes. She approached the kitchen in a rage, looking to take out her anger on Dorothy and me. As soon as Dorothy spotted her standing in the kitchen entryway,

Dorothy dropped the mop and scooped me up into her arms. Dorothy loves me, but sometimes she is overprotective. I had to figure out some way to escape Dorothy's grip and to get the Wicked Witch wet.

Dorothy slowly backed into a corner and the Wicked Witch glanced around the kitchen before taking one step inside. She stared at the bucket, at the mop, at us, and then back at the bucket. It was obvious that she was calculating all the possible ways she could get wet and was trying to decide how she could safely navigate through the kitchen. She thought she could avoid the water by just being careful; she believed that we were both unaware of her fear of water. She took one step towards us and paused when Dorothy's shoes caught her eye. They were the shoes that Star Lady had given to Dorothy. The shoes must be magical because they have protected Dorothy since she put them on her feet.

The Wicked Witch cautiously inched her way by the bucket of water until she was a safe distance away from it. Then, she bolted towards us. Dorothy was startled and threw her head back, hitting it against the wall. This was my chance to escape. Dorothy grabbed her head and started crouching down, holding me in one arm. As Dorothy was about to sit on the floor, the Wicked Witch leaned over us and grabbed Dorothy by the hair to pull her to her feet. Dorothy kicked up her leg, hitting the Wicked Witch's chin. The Wicked Witch's teeth clenched together. Then, she gasped as one of Dorothy's shoes fell off. It landed right in the Wicked Witch's hands.

I looked up at Dorothy's face. She still was holding her head and tears were beginning to fill her eyes. I had to do something. No one can upset Dorothy and get away with it when I'm around. The Wicked Witch was laughing with satisfaction about her victory. Luckily, Dorothy had loosened her hold on me so I leaped out of Dorothy's arms and straight at the Wicked Witch. I bit her leg. Yuck! The taste was awful. I bit her as hard as I could, but the Witch did not bleed. I will never forget the nasty taste of dried blood and old skin. I assumed that she was so wicked that her blood had dried up many years ago because she did not have a heart.

The Wicked Witch fell backwards as she tried to get me to let go of her leg. It was like playing tug of war and I always win at that game. Anyway, I flew into the air over her head as she fell backwards. I landed on my feet right next to the bucket of water. As the Wicked Witch was just about to stand up, I quickly jumped into the bucket, tipping it over. Water spilled out, drenching the Wicked Witch. Then I shook off, spraying more water onto the Wicked Witch. She gazed at me with a dark and cold facial expression. I knew with certainty she wanted to do away with me. She struggled to her feet, slipping on the wet floor. She tried to lunge at me but she was unable to move her legs. Thick black smoke started coming out of her feet. It soon consumed half of her body. This smoke was strange. It didn't have an odor and was confined to the Wicked Witch. Suddenly, the Wicked Witch appeared to be shrinking. Soon her face was melting like a wax candle.

Shocked, Dorothy and I just stared at the Wicked Witch as she melted and disappeared. I could not believe my eyes. She was really melting into nothingness. Then the smoke vanished quickly into the floor and the Wicked Witch was gone. Dorothy slowly stood up and wiped the tears from her eyes. She grabbed the mop and carefully poked the Wicked Witch's remaining clothes with the mop handle. Seeing that the Wicked Witch had really melted away into nothing, I sniffed the residue, confused yet proud. Dorothy drew another bucket of water and threw it over the residue. After that, Dorothy carefully picked out the shinny shoe, which was all that was left of the Wicked Witch besides her hat and cape. Then I decided to do my business on top of the spot where she melted to make sure she was truly gone. Dorothy giggled and after I had finished, she cleaned up the entire mess.

Later, Dorothy cleaned and dried her shoe before putting it back on her foot. There was a brief silence as we tried to process the last few minutes. However, when we both came to the realization that we were free, we bolted outside to get the key and free Big Cat. As the three of us walked back inside, Dorothy told Big Cat what had happened to the Wicked Witch. I especially liked how she motioned every action with her entire body.

CHAPTER 9

THE FETCH

O nce inside, Big Cat and I gathered the raccoon-faced creatures together into the kitchen. This was fun because as soon as I barked they started running, so I just had to make sure they ran in the right direction by running in front of them if they were headed the wrong way. Dorothy made sure that once we got them into the kitchen they didn't leave while we gathered the rest.

When all the raccoon-faced creatures were together, Dorothy stepped onto the kitchen stool and made an announcement. By the way they threw their arms into the air with joy, I figured that she told them that they no longer needed to fear or obey the Wicked Witch. Dorothy waited until the room quieted down before speaking again. Once she had their attention, she stuttered a few times as tears started streaming down her face. She couldn't seem to verbally communicate what she was trying to tell them. Just as she put her head down in sadness, all the raccoon faced creatures got down on their knees with their heads bowed and arms stretched straight out. I put my paw on Dorothy's shoe and she looked up. I guess they were trying to show Dorothy that they were willing to help her in any way they could because they were grateful to her. Dorothy took a deep breath and started making her second announcement. I couldn't understand what she was saying so I stopped trying. The pointing and hand motions being exchanged were very confusing so I laid down. There was pointing everywhere. However, there was significant pointing towards a door by the raccoon-faced creatures. Then, I heard Dorothy call my name, "Toto!" I sprang to my feet and followed everyone outside.

We walked for quite a while in surroundings that seemed to be familiar. I concentrated on keeping up with the others rather than looking at our fast-changing environment. Luckily, they stopped so I could rest my paws and catch my breath. I looked around. I knew where we were because I could recognize the scent of these woods. I was confused. I knew why we were here! Dorothy wanted to come to the place where Metal Man lay dented and immobile to try to rescue him.

Dorothy and the raccoon-faced creatures cautiously made their way down to Metal Man as I watched from the edge of the steep rocky incline. They carried him up, being careful not to harm him further. I continued to watch curiously. As soon as they climbed back over the edge, three of the raccoon-faced creatures carried Metal Man to the castle. Dorothy and the others sat down to rest. I wondered what they were going to do to Metal Man. Suddenly; I got a whiff of Straw Chew Man as he smelled like the horses back in Kansas. I started running in circles, barking until Dorothy and the others followed me into the woods. My nose led me to a tree. The shirt of Straw Chew Man was covered with pine needles. Dorothy picked it up and scratched my head. My head always goes up when she does that, but this time I spotted more of Straw Chew Man's clothes in the tree. I stood up on my hind legs and barked until Dorothy saw the clothes.

Dorothy and the others gathered up as much as they could find of Straw Chew Man. I helped where I could with finding clothes and straw. Then we walked back to the castle with the items we had found. The other raccoon-faced creatures were locked inside the room that everyone was pointing to before. I could hear banging and drilling sounds coming from inside. The creatures that were with us grabbed everything Dorothy and Big Cat were holding. Someone inside let them in the noisy room, making sure that Dorothy, Big Cat, and I couldn't see what was happening. They locked the door back up and the three of us were left to wait.

Despite the noise, Dorothy, Big Cat, and I must have fallen asleep on the floor while waiting to see what was going to happen because the sound of Metal Man walking towards us awakened me. He tapped Dorothy on the shoulder and she jumped up when she saw both him and Straw Chew Man standing in front of her. I wasn't sure how the raccoon-faced creatures had repaired Metal Man and Straw Chew Man, however I was very happy that we were reunited and glad to see the smile on Dorothy's face. My tail would not stop wagging.

Dorothy stayed up all night talking with our companions, catching them up on the events that had occurred. The following morning, Dorothy sent me to gather the raccoon-faced creatures together again. They were starting to feel comfortable around me so I just had to bark once and they followed me. Dorothy and my other companions took turns hugging them. I had a feeling this was going to be the last time we were going to be together from the frowns everyone had on their faces and the tears in their eyes. The raccoon-faced creatures then pointed to a cabinet. Dorothy went to the Witch's cupboard and opened it. It was filled with food, so Dorothy stuffed her basket with goodies for the rest of our journey. Then, just as she was about to close the cabinet, something caught her eye. It was a crown. She tried it on her own head and surprisingly it fit her exactly! I was curious about this crown. I wondered why the Wicked Witch wore a pointy hat and kept this shimmering crown in a cabinet.

CHAPTER 10

THE RETURN OF THE FLYING MONKEYS

The room became dark and I heard a low rumbling sound coming from outside. It was getting louder. An odor of sour milk and bananas was growing stronger. The monkeys were returning. I started barking and Dorothy picked me up. The raccoon-faced creatures scattered and hid. Soon, Dorothy and I were once again face-to-face with the winged monkeys. I guess Dorothy thought that running away like she tried to do the last time would not do any good. Dorothy stood tall and held her head high. Our three companions were doing the same so I stopped barking and tried to look brave too. The monkeys approached us and surprisingly, bowed down on their knees. Dorothy put me back on the floor but I scurried behind her. I was still wary of these monkeys. Dorothy gently lifted the chin of the biggest monkey, wanting to understand him. The monkey held up three figures and pointed at the crown Dorothy was wearing. Dorothy started to smile. The crown holds a power and when someone puts it on, the flying monkeys grant him or her three wishes. That must have been the reason I was unable to warn Dorothy and my companions of the first arrival of the monkeys. That also must have been what the monkeys were discussing with the Wicked Witch. She must have used her last wish on us. Finally, it was all becoming clear.

Dorothy picked up the basket full of food and scooped me up with her other arm. She walked outside with our three companions by her side. The monkeys closely followed. Once outside, Dorothy nodded and called the largest monkey over to her. Before I knew it, half of the monkeys were lifting my companions and me into the air while the other monkeys swiftly flew off ahead of us. As we flew through the air, I felt a sense of comfort, which I didn't have during our first flight with the monkeys. Suddenly, I noticed that we were heading in the direction of the sparkling city. Dorothy's first wish must have been that we didn't need to make the journey back to the sparkling city on foot. The monkeys were helping us reach the city quicker and easier. A few minutes later, I looked down and to my surprise the land of the Wicked Witch was no longer a dark, cold, and gloomy place. It was slowly being filled with flowers as sunlight slowly warmed the land. Dorothy's second wish must have been that the land of the Wicked Witch be transformed into a warmer, more inviting place. I spotted more of the winged monkeys flying towards the castle, as we were carried over the bulldog-looking creature's house in the middle of all the pathways. They were carrying unfamiliar raccoon-faced creatures, but from their resemblance to the creatures back at the castle, I had the feeling that they were relatives. Dorothy's last wish must have been that the raccoon-faced creatures were reunited with their family members. Dorothy certainly knew how to wish. I would have wished to go back home to Kansas, but Dorothy always thought of how she could help other beings before she thought of herself.

Soon we reached the sparkling city and after the monkeys gently placed us on the ground, they said goodbye. Before long, the monkeys were out of sight. We turned around to face the entrance of the Great Sparkling City.

Chapter 11

THE TRUTH

D orothy took a deep breath of relief and then knocked on the door of the wall. Out came the soldier with the cat-like whiskers, shutting the door behind him. Seeing us surprised him, as his jaw dropped. He pointed to the crown on Dorothy's head and started to stutter. He placed the glasses from his pocket over our eyes and without hesitation opened the door for us.

As it opened, Dorothy happily skipped inside. I was bouncing up and down in her arm, but I didn't mind. I was anxious to return home to Kansas and from the shine in Dorothy's eyes, I knew we were going to soon. However, the creatures that Dorothy and I have encountered on this journey will forever haunt us. The creatures that we have battled will remind us of our strengths and to never lose hope. The creatures that helped us especially our three close friends will remind us that friendship and kindness are very powerful things. They will always stay in our hearts although we were going to return to Kansas soon and say goodbye to them. The obstacles we have overcome, the creatures, the wicked witch, and the magic have taught me lessons that I will carry throughout my life. I learned that I should always trust my instincts and that I was fulfilling my duty to protect Dorothy. I also learned that I cannot take on every battle and that being good sometimes means listening to others. Oz was like a life journey.

When we reached the front of the largest building of the Great Sparkling City, like before, the soldier stopped, turning to face us. He held up his hand, signaling for us to stay. He entered the building leaving us waiting.

A few minutes later, the soldier with the cat-like whiskers returned, letting us in the building. He guided us to the room. As we entered, he remained outside the doorway to the room. As before, the room was pitch black. We cautiously stepped forward. Suddenly, the loud voice asked why we were back. Dorothy stepped forward answering by saying we destroyed the Wicked Witch and came back to get our requests granted. Just then, I got a whiff of food. Without Dorothy noticing, I followed my nose as she argued with the loud voice. By mistake, I walked into someone's leg, startling him or her. The person dropped the sandwich onto the ground and without thinking hit a button turning on the lights.

The loud voice was nothing more than a man speaking into a microphone. The fireball, the melting head, and the beast were simply created from props. As Dorothy and the others realized these facts, they all had extremely disappointed looks on their faces. Noticing the hurt looks, the man walked over to

Dorothy, Straw Chew Man, Metal Man, and Big Cat. I followed.

He first removed the glasses from our eyes. As he did, the sparkles disappeared. The people were led to believe that inside the wall, the Great Sparkling City sparkled so much that eyes needed protection. The man did this to reinforce his image of greatness. In truth, only the wall sparkled while the Great Sparkling City didn't sparkle at all and the glasses created the sparkling.

Next, the man took Straw Chew Man's hand and led him into the next room. A few minutes later, they returned and it was obvious that the straw in Straw Chew Man's head was replaced with new straw. Straw Chew Man had a smile from ear to ear. I knew that his request was granted or that he believed it had been granted.

Then, the man took Metal Man's hand and led him into the same room. I heard a lot of noise before they returned moments later. Metal Man had a new welded spot on his chest. However, he was smiling, too. His request must have also been granted or he, too, believed it had been granted.

Next, the man took Big Cat's hand and led him to the table on the side of the room. He grabbed a bottle filled with a clear liquid and handed it to Big Cat. The man whispered something in Big Cat's ear and without hesitation Big Cat drank the liquid. When he finished, Big Cat had a huge smile on his face like the others.

Dorothy picked me up and waited for our turn. The man thought for a second before calling for the soldier with the cat-like whiskers. He entered the room and they both whispered to each other. The soldier walked into the other room as the man led us out of the building. Before I knew it, the soldier was setting up a balloon. The man must have landed here much like Dorothy and I did, but instead of a house, he landed with a balloon. Seeing him coming down from the sky, the people of this land must have glorified him as they glorified Dorothy and me. Until now, he probably didn't have a reason to leave being that he was viewed as royalty here. However, he wanted to grant Dorothy's request, fulfilling his promise of taking us home. The balloon definitely was a sight for sore eyes.

Chapter 12

THE BALLOON OF
LOST HOPE

The balloon was as colorful as the flowers in this land. As the man climbed into the basket of the balloon, Dorothy turned to face Straw Chew Man, Metal Man, and Big Cat. Each of their eyes began to fill with tears. This was it. This was goodbye. Dorothy and I were finally going home to Kansas. I knew Dorothy was sad to leave our new friends as I felt the same, but still we were both excited to go home.

As Dorothy said goodbye, a large crowd started forming around the balloon. People were coming to see us off. Continuing to carry me in her arms, Dorothy stepped up to the basket of the balloon. She turned to smile at our new friends one last time. Then, suddenly, I heard a noise. Before we could climb in the basket, the balloon started floating higher and higher.

Tears filled Dorothy's eyes and ran down her cheeks as the balloon traveled farther and farther away. It soon disappeared out of sight. She placed me on the ground before leaning her head against our friends.

While Straw Chew Man, Metal Man, and Big Cat comforted Dorothy, I spotted the Direction-giver heading toward the door in the wall. He must have come to the city to see us off. I quickly rushed up to him, barking. Recognizing me, he patted my head until Dorothy and the others caught up. I loved the attention from him.

When Dorothy and the others caught up, I put my paw on Dorothy's shoe. With tears still in her eyes, somehow she understood what I was telling her. Hope of going home wasn't lost. The direction-giver stopped petting me as Dorothy pointed to her shoes and then in different directions. He gestured for us to follow him to the door of the wall. Once outside, he pointed in one direction before he waved goodbye.

Chapter 13

THE STRETCHY MEN

We wasted no time and headed in the direction he pointed. Soon, the colorful flowers near the city were out of sight, as pure white flowers now seemed to be everywhere. In the distance, I could see a beautiful castle.

We rushed toward the castle. However, all of a sudden, I sensed danger so I stopped, giving out a single loud bark. Dorothy and the others paused just before a group of Stretchy Men sprung up from the ground ahead of us. Dorothy took another step forward. She then jumped back as one of the Stretchy Men tried to bop her on the head.

These men were mounted to the ground like plants taking root. Their necks stretched and they used their heads to bop trespassers. They were guarding the castle.

I barked as ferociously as I could when I saw them try to hurt Dorothy. To my surprise, Dorothy didn't seem bothered by it. In fact, she had the look of determination in her eyes. I knew she viewed it as just another obstacle to overcome.

She thought for a moment before getting down on her knees and patting the ground twice. The group of mice we had encountered on our way to the Great Sparkling City quickly gathered in front of Dorothy.

Dorothy pointed at the castle and the mice nodded. Dorothy stood up and the mice scurried ahead of us. The Stretchy Men tried to bop the mice, but the mice were to fast for them. We followed the mice. It was impossible for the Stretchy Men to bop us as they hit their heads on the ground trying to bop the mice and weren't able to spring up fast enough to attempt to bop us.

When we reached safety, the mice nodded before going their own way. Dorothy smiled noticing we had reached the castle. She took a deep breath and knocked on the door.

Chapter 14

THE GOODBYE

A small woman opened the door greeting us kindly. She led us to where Star Lady sat. Everything was pure white.

Star Lady gave us a sweet smile. Dorothy fell to her knees with her hands folded. Star Lady stood up, walking over to Dorothy and gently lifting Dorothy's chin with her hand. Dorothy stood up wiping her tears.

Star Lady pointed to the crown and Dorothy carefully handed it to her. She put it on and once again the monkeys appeared. Star Lady placed the crown in the hands of the largest monkey. It finally allowed the monkeys to be free. They no longer had to obey orders from others. The monkeys were ecstatic, thanking Star Lady before leaving.

Star Lady then turned back to Dorothy. She pointed at Dorothy's shoes and tapped her own shoes together three times. Dorothy had a look of surprise on her face as she picked me up to hold me in her arms. Once again, she turned to face Straw Chew Man, Metal Man, and Big Cat to say goodbye. We were all grateful for the friendship we had built along this journey. They had their hopes realized. Now it was our turn and we couldn't wait to return home.

Dorothy finished her goodbyes and clicked her shoes together three times. Suddenly, a white cloud of smoke swirled around Dorothy and me. It was different from the drain of the sky. It provided a feeling of peace as it picked us up.

Chapter 15

HOME

As quickly as the smoke appeared and swirled around us, it vanished. Dorothy gently put me down. I felt the dry dirt of the ground beneath my paws and I knew we were back in Kansas. Dorothy rubbed her eyes. I placed my paw on her foot to make sure she was alright. Just then, I noticed that her new shoes were gone.

They must have fallen off during our travels. I was relieved that I didn't fall because it was a nice feeling to be home. Dorothy scratched my head before dusting herself off and putting on her old shoes from her basket. I was glad she was alright.

I reconnected with the surroundings as Dorothy finished putting on her shoes. I could see the land touch the sky in all directions. There wasn't one tree on the property. The sun was hot especially with my fur coat. Dust blew with the slightest breeze. I was certain we were back in Kansas. We were home!

Then, I saw the house. It was a lovely sight. The gentleman and his wife must have rebuilt after the drain in the sky picked up the other house. This house looked must stronger. It also had a deck circling the entire house. It was there on the deck that the gentleman and his wife stood up from their chairs, staring at us.

Dorothy stood up and picked me up again. She ran towards the house and we were greeted with open arms. Tears filled everyone's eyes as smiles were exchanged. I whimpered with happiness.

The gentleman and his wife signaled for us to go inside. Dorothy gave me a squeeze and rubbed her face against my head before following the gentleman and his wife inside.

The house had the same layout, except for having larger rooms. The tour ended in Dorothy's new bedroom. The bed was as large as the one in the bedroom of the gentleman and his wife. Dorothy placed me on the bed. I bounced a little as I found a place to sit. She sat besides me and started to pet me.

While Dorothy stroked me, I began to think to myself. As long as we were together, it didn't matter where we were; we made the best of it and our adventures taught us life lessons. I was Dorothy's dog, Toto.

About the Author

S hannon K. Mazurick has loved writing
since a young age. She graduated Avon High
School in 2004 and The University of Saint
Joseph (formerly Saint Joseph College) in 2008.
Mazurick received her Bachelors Degree in English
with a minor in Psychology. In 2013, she received
her Masters Degree in Interactive Media through
Quinnipiac University. She is the proud author of
Poetry As The Year Goes By, Reflective Poetry:
Petals of the Heart, Gemma: The Search for the
Gem, Gemma: The Treasure Hunt With Griffin,
Gemma: The First Day Of School With Honoray,

and <u>Toto's Tale (An Adaptation of L. Frank Baum's The Wonderful Wizard of Oz).</u> Mazurick writes in hopes of illustrating how everyone is an individual and everyone has a purpose in life. She also finds writing as a way to express herself and as a means of reflection. Mazurick enjoys the creative aspect that writing offers. She also likes the creativeness and ability to express oneself that artwork offers. Artwork and writing are both means of communication. Her two poetry books feature two art pieces by Mazurick on the covers. For the three Gemma children's books, she worked with the illustrator to make sure every detail, even the colors, matched her visions. For the cover of <u>Toto's Tale (An Adaptation of L. Frank Baum's The Wonderful Wizard of Oz),</u> a silhouette of a dog is over one of Mazurick's art pieces. Mazurick plans to publish more books in the future.

Printed in the United States
By Bookmasters